CANADIANS IN AMERICA

web enhanced at www.inamericabooks.com

JANICE HAMILTON

LERNER PUBLICATIONS COMPANY / MINNEAPOLIS

Current information and statistics quickly become out of date. That's why we developed **www.inamericabooks.com**, a companion website to the **In America** series. The site offers lots of additional information—downloadable photos and maps and up-to-date facts through links to additional websites. Each link has been carefully selected by researchers at Lerner Publishing Group and is regularly reviewed and updated. However, Lerner Publishing Group is not responsible for the accuracy or suitability of material on websites that are not maintained directly by us. It is recommended that students using the Internet be supervised by a parent, a librarian, a teacher, or another adult.

This book is dedicated to all my cross-border friends: my Canadian friends who have moved to the United States; my American friends who have moved to Canada; my American friends at my summer home in Maine; and my ancestors, who made the move from the United States to Canada 200 years ago.

—JH

Copyright © 2006 by Janice Hamilton

All rights reserved. International copyright secured. No part of this book may be reproduced, stored in a retrieval system, or transmitted in any form or by any means—electronic, mechanical, photocopying, recording, or otherwise—without the prior written permission of Lerner Publishing Group, except for the inclusion of brief quotations in an acknowledged review.

Lerner Publications Company
A division of Lerner Publishing Group
241 First Avenue North
Minneapolis, MN 55401 U.S.A.

Website address: www.lernerbooks.com

Library of Congress Cataloging-in-Publication Data

Hamilton, Janice.
    Canadians in America / by Janice Hamilton.
      p.   cm. — (In America)
    Includes bibliographical references and index.
    ISBN-13: 978-0-8225-2681-0 (lib. bdg. : alk. paper)
    ISBN-10: 0-8225-2681-6 (lib. bdg. : alk. paper)
     1. Canadian Americans–History–Juvenile literature. 2. Canadian Americans–Juvenile literature. 3. Immigrants–United States–Juvenile literature. I. Title. II. Series: In America (Minneapolis, Minn.)
E184.C2H36 2006
973'.0411–dc22
                                                    2005009805

Manufactured in the United States of America
1 2 3 4 5 6 – JR – 11 10 09 08 07 06

Contents

INTRODUCTION 4
Canadians in America

1 • CANADA 6
Canada and Its Beginnings
New France
The Removal of the Acadians
The Quebec Act and the American Revolution
The Flood Begins

2 • IN AMERICA 24
Civil War Years
The Turn of the Century
French Canadians in the United States
The Early Twentieth Century

3 • 1960 TO THE PRESENT 36
Immigration Trends
Life in the United States
Different Values
Franco-Americans
Finding Success in the United States

FAMOUS CANADIAN AMERICANS 54
TIMELINE 60
GLOSSARY 63
THINGS TO SEE AND DO 64
SOURCE NOTES 65
SELECTED BIBLIOGRAPHY 66
FURTHER READING & WEBSITES . . . 67
INDEX 70

INTRODUCTION

In America, a walk down a city street can seem like a walk through many lands. Grocery stores sell international foods. Shops offer products from around the world. People strolling past may speak foreign languages. This unique blend of cultures is the result of America's history as a nation of immigrants.

Native peoples have lived in North America for centuries. The next settlers were the Vikings. In about A.D. 1000, they sailed from Scandinavia to lands that would become Canada, Greenland, and Iceland. In 1492 the Italian navigator Christopher Columbus landed in the Americas, and more European explorers arrived during the 1500s. In the 1600s, British settlers formed colonies that, after the Revolutionary War (1775–1783), would become the United States. And in the mid-1800s, a great wave of immigration brought millions of new arrivals to the young country.

Immigrants have many different reasons for leaving home. They may leave to escape poverty, war, or harsh governments. They may want better living conditions for themselves and their children. Throughout its history, America has been known as a nation that offers many opportunities. For this reason, many immigrants come to America.

Moving to a new country is not easy. It can mean making a long, difficult journey. It means leaving home and starting over in an unfamiliar place. But it also means using skill, talent, and determination to build a new life. The In America series tells the story of immigration to the United States and the search for fresh beginnings in a new country—in America.

web enhanced at www.inamericabooks.com

Canadians in America

Fur traders and missionaries were some of the first people from Canada to set foot in the United States. They began exploring modern-day Michigan in the late 1600s, and some of them put down roots there. The first large group of Canadian immigrants was made up of the Acadians. The Acadians spoke French and lived in the modern-day province of Nova Scotia. They arrived in America between 1755 and 1762, after British colonizers forced them to leave their homes.

Between 1840 and 1900, waves of French-speaking and English-speaking Canadians came to the United States. They came in search of jobs and better economic conditions. More Canadians continued to immigrate throughout the 1900s. They came for educational and professional opportunities, to increase their incomes, to marry Americans, and to join relatives who had immigrated. In the early twenty-first century, about 678,000 people of Canadian birth were living in the United States. In addition, millions who were born in the United States claim Canadian ancestry.

Although Canadian immigrants are plentiful in the United States, they are not always easy to identify. Canadians differ from many other immigrants in that they are well acquainted with U.S. culture. Canadians speak English, and they watch U.S. television and read U.S. magazines. While Canadian immigrants do not stand out in the United States, they have made a tremendous impact on the country. Canadian Americans are entertainers, artists, businesspeople, and athletes. They excel in many different fields, and they contribute a great deal to life in their adopted homeland.

1 CANADA

Canada's provinces and territories stretch from the Atlantic Ocean to the east, the Pacific Ocean to the west, and the Arctic Ocean to the north. Canada shares its southern border with the continental United States. Canada's climate varies from temperate to arctic, and its landscape includes plains, mountains, and lowlands. The capital of Canada is Ottawa.

CANADA AND ITS BEGINNINGS

Canada is the second-largest country in the world, but its population is relatively small. About 32 million people live in Canada. In comparison, more than 295 million people live in the physically smaller United States. Four out of five Canadians live in cities, especially in the Montreal, Toronto, and Vancouver regions. More than 75 percent of Canada's population lives within one hundred miles of the U.S. border.

The border region in Canada is

Jasper National Park is in the province of Alberta. Within the park, Spirit Island rises from Maligne Lake.

a lot like the United States. The east coast is traditionally an area of fishing and farming, while central Canada is heavily populated and industrialized. The interior plains of the U.S. Midwest extend northward into the Canadian prairies, and mountain chains parallel the west coast from Alaska to Mexico.

Canada has a rich culture and history. Its first inhabitants were aboriginal people who came from northeast Asia. These people arrived in North America about fifteen thousand to fifty thousand

The resourceful Abenaki were one of the first peoples to settle in what later became the province of Quebec. They navigated its rivers in canoes crafted from birch trees. These canoe makers poured lots of hot water on the thick birchbark to get it to bend into the shape of canoes.

years ago. They may have crossed the Pacific Ocean by boat, or they may have traveled on a bridge of land that existed for a time between northern Asia and Alaska. Gradually, these migrants settled throughout North, Central, and South America.

The aboriginal people developed a variety of cultures suited to different areas. In Canada's eastern woodlands, some groups lived in permanent settlements and farmed corn, beans, and squash. Others lived by hunting animals, such as deer and rabbits. The people traveled by canoe in summer and on snowshoes in winter. On the western prairies, the native way of life centered around buffalo hunting. The people who lived along the northwest coast fished in the sea and carved masks and totem poles. The people of the Arctic hunted seals and built houses from blocks of ice.

In 1497 King Henry VII of England asked John Cabot to find new lands far to the west of England. Cabot crossed the Atlantic Ocean and discovered waters full of fish off the coast of Newfoundland. Soon fishers from Portugal, Spain, and France were visiting the region's waters every summer. They sometimes exchanged goods with the native people they met.

Between 1534 and 1541, French explorer Jacques Cartier traveled to the Saint Lawrence River. This great waterway leads to the interior of North America. Cartier claimed the region for Catholic France but was ultimately disappointed in what he saw. For many years, few Europeans returned to the area.

In 1604 a small group of men set out from France to set up a fur-trading business. They built a tiny settlement on an island in the Saint Croix River, on the current border between Maine and the province of New Brunswick. The next year, they moved the settlement to Port-Royal (modern-day Annapolis Royal, Nova Scotia) on the Bay of Fundy. They called the region Acadie, or Acadia. This first fur-trading business did not make money, so the group went back to France a few years later.

At Gaspé, near Percé Rock, in the present-day province of Quebec, Jacques Cartier claimed Canada for King Francis I of France.

French explorer Samuel de Champlain went on his first voyage to Canada in 1603.

New France

The second attempt to start a fur-trading business in North America succeeded. In 1608 Samuel de Champlain built a fort at present-day Quebec City, on the Saint Lawrence River. The native people brought furs, especially beaver pelts, to the French traders. The traders then shipped the furs to France, where people made them into hats and other fashionable items. The native people taught the newcomers how to make canoes, collect maple syrup, and make a cedar bark tea that was full of vitamin C. But the natives did not benefit from contact with the Europeans. Many of them died of European diseases, such as measles and smallpox.

New France, the colony Champlain established on the Saint Lawrence, became a permanent settlement. Catholic missionaries came to teach the native people about Christianity, and nuns founded schools and hospitals. But the colony offered few economic opportunities for settlers, and they endured many hardships. By 1649 only about one thousand colonists were living in New France. Eventually, the French government decided to give a boost to the colony's population. Between 1663 and 1673, about eight hundred young French women joined the merchants, soldiers, and other men already in the colony. These women were known as *filles du roi* (king's daughters). They chose husbands and eventually raised the first of many generations of large families. These people called themselves

TO FIND OUT MORE ABOUT THE HISTORY OF CANADA, GO TO WWW.INAMERICABOOKS.COM FOR LINKS.

Canadiens (French for Canadians), and they developed their own identity. They felt that they had little in common with the French.

Meanwhile, the British had established colonies of their own in North America, including Virginia and Massachusetts. In the far north, British merchants set up Hudson's Bay Company in 1670 to compete for the fur trade. The Canadiens wanted to find new sources of furs, so a handful of explorers—along with their aboriginal guides—set out from Montreal, on the

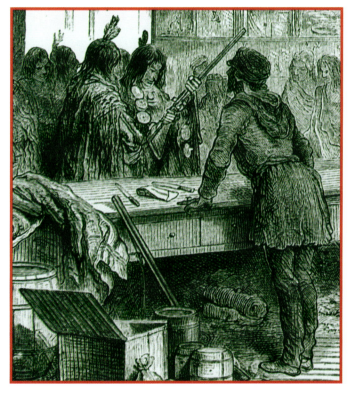

Hudson's Bay Company operated trading posts across North America from 1670 to 1869. The posts traded furs from Native Americans and British colonists for other goods, including weapons and liquor.

Saint Lawrence River. They took a long and difficult journey to the Great Lakes. In 1673 Louis Jolliet and a priest, Jacques Marquette, crossed the Great Lakes and headed south to the Mississippi River. Several years later, René-Robert Cavelier de La Salle traveled down the Mississippi to the Gulf of Mexico.

These *voyageurs* were the first Europeans to live in the region that eventually became Michigan. They established outposts, such as Detroit (1701). Most fur traders visited the region only in the summer, but a few married native women and lived in the area all year.

THE REMOVAL OF THE ACADIANS

While the Canadiens were expanding their colony along the shores of the Saint Lawrence, they also successfully reestablished a settlement in Acadia. The settlers built dikes between the sea and the salt marshes. They farmed the fertile land. But the small colony was in a difficult position. They were caught between the French and the British, who did not get along with one another. The British took control of Acadia in 1713. They renamed it Nova Scotia.

The relationship between the French-speaking, Catholic Acadians and their new British, Protestant governors was strained. The British were worried that the Acadians would side with the French in future conflicts. They asked the Acadians to pledge loyalty to the British king. The Acadians refused. They explained that they wanted to stay neutral (or not side with anyone). But they did promise that they would not

> LEARN MORE ABOUT THE ACADIANS. GO TO WWW.INAMERICABOOKS.COM FOR LINKS.

fight the British. In spite of the tensions between the Acadians and the British, the Acadians made good lives for themselves. Over the next several decades, their population grew to more than twelve thousand.

For many years, the French and the British competed to control the North American colonies and the fur trade. They each built many forts in the 1700s. The British built a fort at Halifax, Nova Scotia. The French had military outposts in northern New York state; Niagara, New York; Detroit, Michigan; and Fort Duquesne, Pennsylvania. The French forts were in excellent locations. But there was a huge territory to defend. The British had two advantages. Their American colonies were far wealthier than New France, and they had a combined population of more than one million. (New France had only fify-five thousand people.)

In the late 1600s, the British fired cannons from Signal Hill (bottom center) *to defend the harbor at Saint John (in modern Newfoundland) from the French.*

By the mid-1700s, both the French and the British had their eyes on the valley surrounding the Ohio River. But they had different visions of the valley's future. The French and their Native American allies wanted to continue trapping wild animals for furs. Settlers expanding westward from Britain's American colonies wanted to farm the land. A French military expedition claimed the Ohio River valley in 1749.

Britain and France were at war with each other off and on for years in the mid-1700s. The Acadians kept their word to remain neutral, but neither the British nor the French really trusted them. Again, the British demanded that the Acadians pledge loyalty to the British king. But the Acadians refused. They did not want to take sides.

A conflict between the British and the French broke out a few years later. It became known as the French and Indian War (1754–1763). On July 28, 1755, the British authorities warned the Acadians that they would expel—or remove—anyone who did not swear loyalty to the king. They immediately started to round up people. They forced the Acadians to board ships and leave their North American homes.

Some Acadians escaped, but about seven thousand people were

In this cartoon from the 1700s, British soldiers have rounded up men in Newfoundland to fight the French.

14

While forcing the Acadians to leave, British soldiers destroyed the homes and property that the Acadians left behind.

forced to leave in the seven years following 1755. British troops burned their homes and farms. Family members were separated. Hundreds died from starvation, disease, or accidental drowning. Those who survived were sent by ship to New York, Pennsylvania, Maryland, North Carolina, South Carolina, and Virginia. There, most of the Acadians lived in desperate conditions and were treated as prisoners of war.

The French and Indian War had another important outcome for North America. The British won a big battle at Quebec City in 1759, and the French surrendered in 1760. In the 1763 treaty (or agreement) that ended the conflict, France handed over all of its

North American territory east of the Mississippi River to Britain. New France became a small British colony along the banks of the Saint Lawrence River. The colony was called Quebec.

Keeping up its North American colonies was costing France a lot of money. So in 1763, France gave the Louisiana Territory (the region drained by the Mississippi River) to Spain. Spain was an ally of France and an enemy of Britain.

The Spanish government said that the Acadians were welcome to move to Louisiana from the American colonies. The first small group of Acadians arrived at the port of New Orleans, Louisiana, in 1764. Several larger groups of Acadians later joined them. In all, about three thousand Acadians settled in Louisiana.

Shortly after the Acadians were expelled from their land, thousands of English-speaking New Englanders moved northward. Some of them took over the farms that had belonged to the Acadians. By the mid-1770s, New Englanders made up 60 percent of Nova Scotia's population of twenty thousand.

THE QUEBEC ACT AND THE AMERICAN REVOLUTION

Although Quebec belonged to the British, few English-speaking settlers moved there. Most people who lived in Quebec spoke French. In 1774 the British passed the Quebec Act. This act officially gave French Canadians the right to speak

Some are for keeping Canada, others [for keeping the Caribbean island of] Guadeloupe. Who will tell me what I shall be hanged for not keeping?

—British prime minister William Pitt's alleged comment after France surrendered Canada to the British in 1763. The British were not sure that they wanted Canada.

This map shows Canada as it appears in modern times. Download this and other maps at www.inamericabooks.com.

French and to practice their Catholic religion. It also expanded Catholic Quebec's territory to the spot where the Ohio and Mississippi rivers meet. The British hoped this would improve their ability to control the fur trade in that region. But the Quebec Act had some negative consequences for the British. In addition to giving rights to French Canadians, the act prevented American settlers from expanding westward into the Ohio region. This upset the settlers. It was one of the factors that led to the American Revolution--the settlers' rebellion against the British, who were in charge of the American colonies at that time.

Settlers involved in the Revolution hoped that the colonies to the north would rebel against the British too. In 1775 a colonial rebel force captured Montreal, Quebec. But most Canadiens were not interested in joining the Revolution. The Americans also tried and failed to capture Quebec City. They left Quebec the following spring when British soldiers arrived.

In Nova Scotia, most people decided not to take sides in the Revolution. Many in Nova Scotia had bad feelings toward the American colonies. Pirates from America's East Coast had invaded Nova Scotia and frightened the people there.

Although Canadiens did not get involved in the American Revolution, the Revolution did have an important consequence for their region.

Pirates from the south frequently attacked Nova Scotia. Settlers there were angry that the American colonies had not stopped these pirates. Some pirate ships flew the Jolly Roger, a flag featuring a skull and crossed bones.

Thousands of Loyalists (people who had fought beside the British) moved north. This was one of the few times when more people moved from the United States to Canada rather than the other way around. The arrival of the Loyalists led to the creation of two new colonies: New Brunswick and Upper Canada (later renamed Ontario).

The Treaty of Paris, the agreement that ended the Revolution, was signed in 1783. It brought peace and established the first border between the British territories and the young United States. For the most part, however, the border meant little. People could cross it easily.

In 1783 Detroit, Michigan, had a population of about two thousand.

After the American Revolution ended, many Loyalists settled at the present site of Saint John, New Brunswick.

Most non-native residents of Detroit were of French Canadian origin. Long, narrow farms, similar to those found in Quebec, lined the banks of the Detroit River. Apple and pear orchards thrived. Farmers sold the extra crops they grew. Social activities in the town centered on family and the Roman Catholic Church. Some of the men enjoyed playing a rough ball game called lacrosse with the Native Americans.

The American Revolution seemed far away. Many of the area's residents considered it to be a conflict between *les anglais* (the English) and *les bostonnais* (the Bostonians). When the Revolution ended, the region officially became U.S. territory. However, the British did not leave their outposts there until 1796.

THE FLOOD BEGINS

In the War of 1812 (1812–1815), the United States declared war on the British. The Americans were annoyed with Great Britain's policies at sea. The Americans tried to invade the British colonies of Lower Canada and Upper Canada. The British forces, with the help of Native American allies and Canadian militia (citizens organized for military service), turned them back. During wartime, trade and the movement of immigrants across the border stopped.

Native Americans of North America invented lacrosse. This game, played with sticks and a ball, is still popular.

BORDER ISSUES

In the 1700s and 1800s, mapmaking was not an exact science. No one knew for sure where the United States ended and Canada began. Many disputes arose about the U.S.-Canadian border. In the 1830s, fights broke out between Maine and New Brunswick loggers. The loggers disagreed over who had the right to cut down trees.

The land disputes continued into the early 1900s. The final disagreement involved the Alaska Panhandle. The Panhandle is a strip of land between northern British Columbia and the Pacific coast. Settling this dispute became particularly important in 1896, when gold was discovered in northern Canada. About one hundred thousand people headed north hoping to make their fortunes. In 1903 a committee with members from both sides gave the Panhandle to the United States. Many Canadians were unhappy with the ruling, since Canada's north lost access to the Pacific.

This 1839 cartoon is about the fight between Maine and New Brunswick loggers. It shows Britain's Queen Victoria (left, holding a shield) *and U.S. president Martin Van Buren* (holding a sword and a shield). *She scolds him for "threaten[ing] a young woman with a war about a few sticks of timber."*

In the United States, the French-speaking communities in Michigan and Louisiana developed in very different ways. After 1825 the completion of the Erie Canal made travel across New York state easier by linking the Hudson River at Albany, New York, to Lake Erie at Buffalo, New York. Many newcomers crossed New York on the Erie Canal to reach Michigan. By the mid-1830s, French Canadians were a minority in the new state of Michigan. They became more and more a part of the general population.

In Louisiana most Acadians established small farms along the bayous (streams) in the southern part of the state. They raised crops and cattle and fished and trapped. Because this area was quite isolated, they were able to preserve many Acadian ways, including their Catholic faith, French language, and simple lifestyle. Eventually, the word *Acadian* became *Cajun*.

The Cajuns were known for their love of life, their friendliness, and their music. They got together often to hold dances. They marked important events such as births, marriages, and deaths. And they helped each other with the harvest. But many of them were very poor. Some people looked down on the Cajuns as ignorant and uneducated.

Change was also occurring in Canada. Both Upper and Lower Canada were ruled by small, elite groups of leaders. Some Canadians wanted this to change. Rebellions broke out in both colonies in

> BEAUTIFUL IS THE LAND, WITH ITS PRAIRIES AND FORESTS OF FRUIT-TREES; UNDER THE FEET A GARDEN OF FLOWERS, AND THE BLUEST OF HEAVENS BENDING ABOVE, AND RESTING ITS DOME ON THE WALLS OF THE FOREST.
> THEY WHO DWELL THERE HAVE NAMED IT THE EDEN OF LOUISIANA.
>
> —Henry Wadsworth Longfellow, "Evangeline" (1847), inspired by Acadians' experiences in Louisiana

The Underground Railroad

Between about 1840 and 1860, thousands of African Americans used a network of safe routes and shelters to flee slavery (which was legal in the southern United States). People called this network the Underground Railroad. Slaves made their way to safety in the northern states or to Canada, where slavery was not allowed. At least thirty thousand people used the Underground Railroad to reach Canada.

1837 and 1838. When the rebellions failed, some of the rebel leaders fled to the United States, although most later returned.

Worried that the rebellions would hurt their economy, many Canadians left for the United States. Once this flood of immigration started, it seldom slowed. In 1853 the Grand Trunk Railway was completed between Montreal and Portland, Maine. Many immigrants packed their belongings into suitcases and boarded trains, bound for new lives in the United States.

2 IN AMERICA

The 1860s marked an important turning point in Canada's history. The country began to develop and grow. But Canadians had a hard time finding work. Manufacturing jobs were scarce, and eastern Canada had run out of land to farm. Canadians began moving to the United States in larger numbers. They sought better jobs, higher incomes, and greater opportunity.

CIVIL WAR YEARS

The U.S. Civil War (1861–1865) had an impact on Canada's growth. During the Civil War, the Union (Northern states, where slavery was illegal) fought the Confederacy (Southern states, which withdrew from the Union to keep slavery legal). Britain sided with the Confederacy. Canada was still a British colony. As a result, tensions grew between Canada and the United States. Some Canadians worried that the Union would attack them.

The Civil War taught Canadians that they needed to become stronger

Canadians who fought in the Civil War

U.S. soldiers weren't the only ones who fought in the Civil War. Some Canadians did too. No one knows exactly how many Canadians enlisted, but at least twenty thousand did. Even outside of the United States, opinions on the war were divided. While the British favored the Confederacy, many Canadians were strongly opposed to slavery. Most Canadians who enlisted signed up with the Union army.

so that they wouldn't be as vulnerable to attacks. Some of the colonies decided to form a union. In 1840 Upper Canada and Lower Canada had merged to form the Province of Canada. In 1867 Nova Scotia and New Brunswick, together with the Province of Canada, formed the Dominion of Canada.

The Canadian west opened to settlement. The government signed treaties with the native people of the plains. Canadian leaders promised money and other benefits in exchange for ownership of the land. The Canadian Pacific Railroad brought settlers to the prairies. But the prairies were more isolated and lonely, and they did not attract large numbers of settlers.

The situation was different in eastern Canada. Many people lived there, so there wasn't enough land for farming. Farmers had a hard time supporting their families. Things weren't any easier for those looking for jobs. At the end of the nineteenth century, Canada still had only five small cities. Few jobs were available in industries such as manufacturing. Jobs were much easier to come by in the United States. U.S. workers made more money too. Even in Ontario,

Canada's richest province, average income levels were well below those in the United States. Many Canadians were drawn south of the border. They came to find jobs in logging, mining, textiles, and other industries.

The Turn of the Century

No one knows exactly how many people came to the United States from Canada. One source estimated that 1.5 million immigrants arrived before 1900. Most immigrants did not have far to move. Many Canadians lived close to the border, and four-fifths of Canadian immigrants settled in northern states.

By 1900 Canadians represented 11 percent of the foreign-born population of the United States. Only German and Irish immigrants outnumbered them. Large Canadian communities existed in Detroit, Michigan; Buffalo, New York; Boston, Massachusetts; Chicago, Illinois; and Seattle, Washington. One in five people born in Canada was living in the United States.

In their national anthem, "O Canada," English Canadians pledge to love their "home and native land" and French Canadians to honor the "terre de nos aïeux"—the land of their ancestors. Between 1870 and 1900, more than a million Canadians broke that pledge, including Calixa Lavallée, the composer of the song.

— John Herd Thompson and Stephen J. Randall, Canada and the United States: Ambivalent Allies, *2002*

Although many of these immigrants came from rural areas, they usually settled in U.S. towns and cities. The men generally found jobs in services, such as banks, stores, and schools, or in manufacturing.

Immigration via Canada

Immigrants from Europe and other regions around the world often sailed directly from their home countries to ports in the United States. Others, however, went to Canada first. From there, they entered the United States by land. In the summer, most arrived at the ports of Montreal or Quebec City on the Saint Lawrence River. In the winter, when the Saint Lawrence River was frozen, they docked at Halifax, Nova Scotia, or Saint John, New Brunswick. The U.S. government has no entry records for those who arrived this way during the nineteenth century.

In the late 1880s, the U.S. government started to tighten immigration rules for people arriving at its ports. To gain easier entry to the United States, more and more immigrants chose the Canadian route. They included people from Ireland, Sweden, Norway, Russia, Italy, Greece, and other Mediterranean countries. Some immigrants stayed in Canada for months or years before moving to the United States. Some had children born in Canada.

In 1894 the United States set up a system to count and control these immigrants. Steamship lines that brought people from Europe, as well as railway companies that carried them across the border, agreed to carry only passengers who were eligible to enter the United States. The U.S. Immigration Service stationed inspectors at Canadian ports. By 1906 they also were inspecting people crossing at land border points.

Many Canadian men worked in the iron and steel industries of the eastern and midwestern United States. Others had jobs in the industries that manufactured agricultural tools and vehicles. Only one in five farmed.

FRENCH CANADIANS IN THE UNITED STATES

French Canadian immigrants settled primarily in New England and Michigan. Michigan was much farther from Quebec than New England. To reach it, people had to travel by train, then take a steamship across the Great Lakes. Nevertheless, it attracted people because of its historical connection to New France.

The peak period of French Canadian immigration was 1860 to 1900. French Canadian immigrants faced many obstacles. Many were illiterate, but a number of them learned to read after they arrived in the United States. The majority were poor and lived in crowded apartment buildings. The children often did not get enough nutritious food to eat. Many Americans looked down on French Canadians because they

This 1890s photo shows how a steel mill in Homestead, Pennsylvania, filled the air with thick, dirty smoke. Immigrants from Canada as well as many other countries worked in U.S. steel mills.

GO TO WWW.INAMERICABOOKS.COM TO FIND MORE INFORMATION ABOUT FRENCH CANADIAN COMMUNITIES IN THE UNITED STATES.

worked for low wages and did not speak English.

Most of the French-speaking Canadians who moved to New England were from Quebec, but some were Acadians from the East Coast. They usually moved into communities that became known as *p'tit Canada* (Little Canada) or Frenchville, in factory towns such as Lowell, Massachusetts, and Lewiston, Maine. The 1900 census showed that large numbers of French Canadians were living in several states: Massachusetts (134,416), New Hampshire (44,420), Rhode Island (31,533), Maine (30,908), and New York (27,199).

Often just a few members of a family immigrated first to explore the opportunities in a community. Brothers, sisters, cousins, and others later followed. Many thought of the move as temporary. All were determined to maintain their culture and their language. They built churches with tall steeples that reminded them of home. French-speaking priests looked after their spiritual needs and kept track of their births and deaths in church records. They shopped at stores run by French Canadians. They also had their own schools, newspapers, and community organizations.

Both men and women worked in New England's textile mills and so did children. Working conditions were poor. The machines in the mills were hot and extremely noisy.

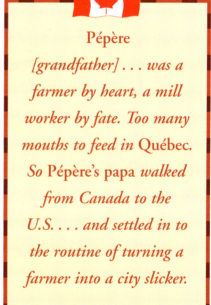

Pépère [grandfather] . . . *was a farmer by heart, a mill worker by fate. Too many mouths to feed in* Québec. *So* Pépère's papa *walked from Canada to the U.S. . . . and settled in to the routine of turning a farmer into a city slicker.*

—Rhea Côté Robbins, a Canadian American author describing her French Canadian ancestors in Wednesday's Child, 2001

Cotton dust was everywhere, and it got into the workers' lungs. Workers labored in the mills for ten or more hours each day. They often worked six days a week.

In Michigan, French Canadians maintained strong cultural traditions for many years. French Canadians had their own churches, schools, newspapers, and

NEW ENGLAND PAROCHIAL SCHOOLS

The French Canadians who moved to the United States were determined to maintain their heritage, language, and religious beliefs. One way they did this was to send their children to French-language schools that were run by the Catholic Church.

The first such parochial, or religious, school was founded by a Montreal-based order of nuns in Rutland, Vermont, in 1870. A few years later, parochial schools opened in Fall River, Massachusetts, and Lewiston, Maine. Parents paid fifty cents per month for each child. These schools became central to community activities. Everyone in the church came to the school Christmas plays and musical performances.

For many French Canadian students, education began and ended in parochial school. Most of the children did not go on to high school or college. Those who did usually went to boarding school in Canada or New England.

By around 1912, the parochial schools began teaching a bilingual program. Half of the subjects were taught in English, and the other half were taught in French.

In front of Detroit's city hall, Tigers baseball fans await the final score in the 1908 American League playoffs. The U.S. Census reports that Detroit's population was more than 400,000 in 1900. As many as 15,000 of Detroit's residents may have been French Canadians or descendents of French Canadians.

community organizations. In 1900 French Canadians were the fourth-largest immigrant group in Michigan. They made up 3.6 percent of the state's population. About 34,500 foreign-born French Canadians and 55,000 individuals born in Michigan of French Canadian parents lived in the state.

In Louisiana change began to creep into the isolated, French-speaking Cajun communities after 1900, when oil was discovered there. Some Cajuns got jobs at oil refineries. Then the state government passed a law saying that all children had to attend school. Everyone had to speak English in school. Teachers punished children for speaking French.

THE EARLY TWENTIETH CENTURY

In spite of the hardships Canadian immigrants faced, they usually found success in their new home. A U.S. Senate commission studying immigrant workers between 1908 and 1911 found that the average weekly earnings of Canadian men aged eighteen and over were well above those of other foreign-born workers ($14.15, compared with $11.92) and only slightly less than those of white U.S. workers. Canadian immigrants contributed a great deal to industry in the United States. They worked hard and helped the U.S. economy.

While the spike in Canadian immigration benefited the United States, it caused hardships for Canada. Canada's population dropped. The loss of so many energetic young men and women made it difficult for Canada to create a strong economy. But in the early twentieth century, Canada became a popular destination for immigrants from Europe. Canada's population began to grow. Newcomers from Russia, Poland, and Ukraine began farming on the prairies. They joined the Native Americans (whose population had decreased due to European diseases) and the Métis, the descendants of Europeans and Native Americans.

Many Canadians fought in World War I (1914–1918). But the war did not stop Canadians from coming to the United States. Approximately 375,000 Canadians immigrated during the war. Immigration continued in the 1920s. Canadian

In a World War I battle, Canadian soldiers scramble out of their battle trench to attack German soldiers.

This map of Canadian American population centers and other maps are downloadable at www.inamericabooks.com.

workers were attracted by a booming U.S. economy. The U.S. government passed laws limiting immigration in the 1920s. But these laws did not apply to Canadians. Among the talented Canadians who came to the United States in the 1920s were university graduates, mechanics, and people with professional skills.

U.S. government studies reveal a great deal about Canadian immigrants between 1906 and 1930. More than half (57 percent) were men, and 43 percent were women. The majority were between the ages of fifteen and forty-four. About 57 percent of the men were single, while there were an equal number of married and single women. Many families with young children also made the move. Most could read and write, although a higher proportion of

English-speaking Canadians (97 percent) than of French Canadians (79 percent) were literate. British Canadian male immigrants included businesspeople, engineers, managers, students, and carpenters.

Of the women who immigrated, 62 percent declared they had no occupation or worked as homemakers. The one in three women who did work outside the home often took jobs in teaching and nursing or were nursing students. Most of the single women traveled alone to the United States.

The Great Depression was a time of economic hardship that began in 1929. Economic activity slowed around the world. Many Canadians lost their jobs in the United States. Some decided to return to their homeland. Immigration also slowed during World War II (1939–1945). Canadian industries hired workers to

Men and women make weapons in this factory in Saskatchewan during World War II.

produce war supplies, and many Canadians fought in the armed forces. Right after the war, however, immigration from Canada rose again.

When logging declined in Michigan, some people got jobs in the new automobile industry. But many lumberjacks moved to Wisconsin or Minnesota. New immigrant groups arrived from Europe and, by 1950, French Canadians were only the ninth-largest group in Michigan. Many of their churches and newspapers closed as people gradually became part of the U.S. way of life.

In Louisiana the Cajuns were also gradually becoming part of the mainstream. New bridges and highways ended their isolation. Radios and telephones connected the bayous to the world. Television became popular in the 1950s, bringing even more U.S. influences to the Cajuns.

While French-speaking Canadians took time to become part of U.S. society, Canadians who spoke English did not have a long adjustment. They faced no communication barrier, and they shared many aspects of U.S. culture. They were "hidden immigrants" because they merged so well into U.S. life. In many cases, even their friends may not have realized that they were not born in the United States. They did not have their own newspapers, churches, or other social organizations. They did not dominate any particular industries.

In the first half of the twentieth century, Canadians usually moved to communities where close family members had already settled. The family members helped them find housing and jobs. The immigrants generally chose areas in the United States that were similar in climate and landscape to the regions they had left. For example, two out of three immigrants from Ontario moved to either Michigan or New York. Most of those who left British Columbia went to neighboring Washington State or to Oregon, California, or Montana. Industrial areas of Massachusetts were the choice of half of the immigrants from eastern Canada.

3 1960 TO THE PRESENT

Throughout the twentieth century, many Canadians came to the United States in search of new opportunities. Canadian immigration continues in the twenty-first century. While Canadian immigrants merge easily into U.S. society, they do encounter stumbling blocks in their new homes. But Canadian Americans are determined to achieve their goals. Through hard work and dedication, they can find success in the United States.

IMMIGRATION TRENDS

In the early 1960s, about fifty thousand Canadians headed south of the border each year. Those who left were often well educated. Canadians were concerned about the high immigration rate among the educated. They worried that Canada was losing its most promising residents. Canadians referred to the loss of their country's educated citizens as the "brain drain."

In 1965 the United States limited the number of annual immigrants from any country, including Canada, to twenty thousand individuals. At the same time, the United States was becoming less appealing to Canadians. The 1960s were a difficult decade in the United States. Tensions between blacks and whites led to race riots. The country was facing economic problems. And the Vietnam War (1957–1975), a controversial conflict in Southeast Asia, brought out protesters across the country. For several years, the flow of immigrants reversed directions. American men who did not want to fight in Vietnam, as well as other disillusioned Americans, fled to Canada. Between 1970 and 1979, 193,000 Americans moved to Canada, while 180,000 Canadians moved to the United States.

In 1969 young Canadians throw a Christmas party for American men who live in Montreal, Quebec, Canada. These men moved to Canada to avoid fighting in Vietnam.

During the 1980s, the trend shifted back to the north-to-south pattern. About fifteen thousand to twenty thousand Canadians came to live in the United States each year. During the 1990s, a strong U.S. economy attracted twenty-eight thousand people from Canada every year. (This figure includes twenty thousand individuals born in Canada and eight thousand born elsewhere but traveling from Canada.) Canadian university graduates, including nurses, librarians, and engineers, settled in Texas, New York, Florida, California, and other states. An estimated three hundred thousand Canadians currently live in northern California, where many work for high-tech companies.

In the past, most immigrants from Canada had to apply to be permanent residents of the United States. That changed after the North American Free Trade Agreement (NAFTA) went into effect in 1994. Under NAFTA, Canadians in certain professions who are offered jobs can easily get temporary visas allowing them to work in the United States. The visa can be renewed every year, but a new visa is needed if the person changes jobs. Professionals qualifying for these temporary visas include accountants, architects,

North American leaders sign NAFTA, standing, left to right, Mexican president Carlos Salinas de Gortari, U.S. president George H. W. Bush, and Canadian prime minister Brian Mulroney. Seated, left to right, are trade representatives Jaime Serra Puche (Mexico), Carla Hills (United States), and Michael Wilson (Canada).

engineers, hotel managers, lawyers, librarians, dentists, and physicians. Some Canadians renew their visas over and over. Others, such as people who marry U.S. citizens, can become permanent residents and, eventually, citizens. Still others choose to return to Canada. They may become disappointed with life in the United States, or have family- or career-related reasons for returning.

Many Canadians remain in the United States as permanent residents for many years without becoming citizens. In fact, less than half of Canadian-born immigrants (about 43 percent) are U.S. citizens. A large majority of them arrived in the United States before 1980. Apart from being able to vote in U.S. elections, many Canadians do not see much benefit in becoming U.S. citizens. And some want to remain different from their U.S. neighbors. But others become citizens to show their gratitude for the opportunities and benefits they have experienced in the United States.

Life in the United States

As a group, recent immigrants from Canada do not have much difficulty adjusting to life in the United States. They quickly make a place for themselves in their adopted country. One reason they integrate so rapidly is that they often find jobs soon after immigrating. Because the immigrants speak English and are familiar with U.S. culture, employers are eager to hire them.

In the early twenty-first century, more than 80 percent of Canadian Americans aged twenty-five to fifty-four worked outside of the home. Almost half of those were employed as managers or other professionals. One in four had careers in technical fields, sales, and administrative support (that is, managing offices and assisting office staff). Less than 1 percent were unemployed.

Canadian immigrants also enjoy economic success. In the early twenty-first century, the average income of Canadian-born households was $46,799 a year compared to $41,733 a year for immigrants from Europe. Of 343,000 Canadian American households, 14 percent had total incomes of $15,000 to $24,999, and 44 percent earned between $25,000 and $74,000. Just over 25 percent had incomes over $75,000 a year. Canadian immigrants find economic success in part because of their high education levels. About 85 percent of them are high school graduates, and 36 percent have at least one college degree. The age at which Canadians come to the United States also contributes to their success. About half of them are between the ages of twenty-five and fifty-four. These are important years when people advance their careers and raise their families.

Despite their success in the United States, Canadian immigrants do face challenges when they arrive in their new home. Those who want to purchase homes sometimes find it difficult. To buy homes, most people must borrow money from banks. In order to borrow money, they often have to answer questions about their finances. They must show that they have good financial histories. Often, even Canadians with excellent financial histories are not allowed to borrow money. Because they have no financial history in the United States, many banks won't give them loans.

Without a U.S. financial history, some Canadian Americans have found it difficult to buy homes in the United States.

Some Canadian immigrants also find themselves feeling homesick. And if they want to share their feelings with other Canadian Americans, it can be difficult for them to spot each other. Few restaurants feature Canadian food, so they cannot easily bond over meals from their home country. One way they reach out to one another is by visiting clubs especially for Canadian immigrants. These clubs are usually found in U.S. cities with large Canadian populations. One such gathering place is the Canadian Club in New York City. It hosts social activities and sponsors fundraising events for charities. In other cities, Canadian Americans read newsletters or websites designed to put Canadians in touch with one another. They might also attend concerts or films featuring Canadian or Canadian American stars.

Canadian American actor Jim Carrey played Count Olaf in the 2004 U.S. film Lemony Snicket's A Series of Unfortunate Events.

In a National Hockey League game, a Toronto Maple Leafs goalie (right) *blocks a shot by a player on the Philadelphia Flyers. Many Canadian American hockey fans enjoy games between Canadian and U.S. teams the most.*

Like native-born Americans, many Canadian immigrants find fellowship at sporting events. Hockey is the favorite sport of many Canadians. In U.S. cities with National Hockey League teams, Canadian Americans often run into each other at games—especially when Canadian teams visit.

Holidays give Canadian Americans another reason to get together. Many Canadian Americans celebrate Canada Day each July 1 by hanging a Canadian flag on their front porch and inviting friends for a backyard barbecue. The other traditional get-together is Canadian Thanksgiving, which is observed in October. Canadians eat big turkey dinners and enjoy pumpkin pies for dessert—much like Americans do at their Thanksgiving celebrations. French Canadians keep family traditions alive at Christmas. Even young children stay up past midnight on Christmas Eve to open presents and eat pork pies called *tortières*.

The holidays aren't the only times Canadians enjoy traditional foods. Many Canadian Americans prepare familiar dishes to keep in touch with their roots. They also beg friends and relatives back home to send their favorite candy bars and other treats that are not available in the United States.

While Canadian cooking is extremely varied, one traditional food many Canadians enjoy is shepherd's pie. This hearty meat pie with a mashed-potato crust makes a perfect meal during Canada's cold winter months. Grilled-cheese sandwiches are another mealtime staple in Canada. Canadian Americans don't have any trouble finding this traditional food in their new country. In Quebec *poutine* is a favorite. This snack of french fries and cheese curds drenched in gravy is hard to find in the United States. And Canadians across the country eat Nanaimo bars, a rich dessert named after the city of Nanaimo on Vancouver Island.

Shepherd's pie is a traditional Canadian food.

Many Canadian Americans–especially those who immigrated to Canada before moving on to the United States–enjoy foods that reflect Canada's ethnic diversity. Indian, Thai, and Lebanese cooking are popular in Canada. Modern Canadian cuisine includes everything from couscous (a grain commonly used in North African cooking) to bok choy (a leafy vegetable found in Asian dishes).

BANNOCK

Bannock is a type of bread. It was a staple in the diets of early settlers in Canada. Canadians sometimes make bannock over a campfire as a summertime treat. They often add ingredients such as raisins, nuts, or fresh blueberries. To learn how to prepare other Canadian dishes, visit www.inamericabooks.com for links.

4 c. flour
4 tsp. baking powder
1 tsp. salt

1½ c. water
3 tbsp. corn oil

1. Preheat oven to 400°F.
2. Put the dry ingredients in a bowl. Add the water slowly, mixing constantly.
3. Pick up the ball of dough and place it on a floured countertop or cutting board. Sprinkle a little flour on your hands and knead the dough, turning it over and over until all the ingredients are well mixed, or about 10 minutes. The dough should not feel wet.
4. Shape the dough into biscuits about ¾-inch thick.
5. Coat a cookie sheet with some of the corn oil. Place the biscuits on the cookie sheet and brush a little oil on top.
6. Bake the biscuits for about 10 minutes, or until they are golden brown. Turn them over and bake about 10 more minutes.
7. The bannock is cooked when a toothpick or knife comes out of the center clean. Bannock may be eaten hot or cold, with butter and jam.

Serves 4

Some Canadians never look back after they settle in the United States. But most maintain ties with friends and relatives in Canada. Many travel to Canada or welcome visitors from home during vacation periods or long weekends. This is particularly easy for those who live near the border. Many families have had close ties across the border for generations. Some people who live right on the boundary line even have to stop at the Customs and Immigration office before they visit their neighbors!

THE 51ST STATE?

Many people want closer ties between the United States and Canada. They think the border between the two countries should be more open. Someday, closer relations may become a reality.

Some predict that the Canada-U.S. border will practically disappear by 2025. Then people could drive across the border without stopping, and Canadians and Americans would have the right to live or work in either country. A few people even think Canada might one day join the United States.

Others think that the border between the two countries will tighten. In 2005 the U.S. Department of Homeland Security announced that Canadians and returning U.S. travelers will soon need passports to cross the border into the United States. Some observers worry that this means the relationship between the United States and Canada is souring. Historically, the United States' northern border has been easy to cross.

Different Values

Since Canada is so closely tied to the United States, Canadian immigrants sometimes have a hard time maintaining their own identity. Canadians have always had difficulty identifying cultural characteristics that are uniquely Canadian. For many, being a Canadian simply means not being an American. But many differences exist between the two societies.

One of the biggest differences is religion. Only about 22 percent of Canadians say that they attend a religious service once a week, while

Canadian Traits and Traditions

Canadians are similar to Americans in many ways, but they do some things differently. Here are a few traits that separate Canadians from their neighbors to the south:

- In Canada people sometimes end their sentences with the expression *eh*. For example, a Canadian might say, "Nice weather today, eh?"
- Instead of salt or ketchup, Canadians often put vinegar on their french fries.
- Canadians celebrate Canada Day, their national birthday, on July 1, just a few days before the Fourth of July. They often display their nation's flag on this day and attend picnics, outdoor concerts, fireworks displays, and parades. In general, however, Canadians tend to be embarrassed by big demonstrations of patriotism.

about 42 percent of Americans say they do. One study found that 59 percent of Americans say religion is important to them compared to 30 percent of Canadians. Furthermore, religion and politics tend to be more closely connected in the United States than they are in Canada. Some Canadians who move to the United States are uncomfortable with this difference.

Some Canadian immigrants have a hard time adapting to the competitive nature of U.S. society, especially in big cities such as New York and Los Angeles. An even bigger adjustment is paying for their own health care. In Canada, the government provides many services to people in need.

> THERE AREN'T A LOT OF THINGS ONTO WHICH YOU CAN PIN A DISTINCTIVELY CANADIAN CULTURE, OTHER THAN GROWING UP AND LEARNING THAT YOU'RE CANADIAN AND NOT AMERICAN.
>
> —Mark Snyder, Canadian immigrant and psychologist at the University of Minnesota, quoted in Jeffrey Simpson's *Star-Spangled Canadians: Canadians Living the American Dream, 2000*

U.S. seniors protest a drug company's prescription drug prices. Immigrants from Canada are not used to the high cost of health care in the United States.

Canadian Immigrants: True Stories

Kathleen Fell, twelve, was just seven when her family moved from Canada to Texas. They left when her father got a job in Dallas. Kathleen says that many Texans think she has an accent, but they don't tease her about it. "They think it is cool," she explains. Kathleen misses the snow, and she misses her relatives back in Canada. But she likes Texas. She and her brother go to a good public school, and her father enjoys his job in the airline industry. The Fells have become permanent residents of the United States. Still, Kathleen would like to return to Canada someday to attend college there.

Jacques Geoffrion moved from Montreal to the United States to marry an American. He also hoped to pursue a television career. Jacques's career changed directions, and his marriage didn't last—but he is very happy in the United States. He lives in San Francisco, California, with his son,

For many immigrants, the Golden Gate Bridge in San Francisco symbolizes the good life they hope to find in the United States.

his second wife, and his stepdaughter. Jacques still maintains close ties to Canada. He and his son sometimes go to hockey games, especially when the Montreal Canadiens are visiting. And every few years, the family spends a white Christmas with relatives in Montreal. Even when they spend the holidays at home in the United States, they stay up late on Christmas Eve to celebrate in traditional French Canadian style.

Robin Dosonge was fourteen and in ninth grade when he and his mother left their home north of Montreal to live in rural Florida. They moved to join Rob's future stepfather. It wasn't an easy move for Rob. "I was the new kid in town," he says. His classmates made fun of the way he talked and asked him whether he lived in an igloo. Rob joined the army's Reserve Officers' Training Corps at school because the kids weren't allowed to make fun of him there. After high school, Rob went to college in Orlando. He hopes to get a job with a wireless communications company.

Canadian immigrants also must adjust to the high cost of a U.S. college education. College is not as expensive in Canada. Most Canadians are aware of these differences before they immigrate to the United States. But it still takes time for them to adjust, and some eventually decide to return to their native country.

Canada and the United States also differ on attitudes toward home and family. When asked whether they believe that the father of the family must be the master of the home, almost 50 percent of Americans agreed. Only 18 percent of Canadians did. Attitudes toward violence differ too. Almost 25 percent of Americans accept violence as part of everyday life. Only 12 percent of Canadians agree with them. The United States has higher crime rates than Canada. This frightens many Canadians who are considering moving to the United States.

Franco-Americans

Modern immigrants of French Canadian descent have slipped into U.S. society with the same ease as other Canadians. Most descendants of French Canadian immigrants identify themselves as Americans or Franco-Americans (Americans from a French-speaking background). While the name shows how comfortable French Canadians feel in the United States, it also shows that they have lost some of their traditional culture.

In New England, Franco-Americans preserved their language and culture for several generations. But even this community's cultural identity has faded over time.

> **America honors the lone warrior fighting for truth and justice . . . Canada honors compromise, harmony, and equality. Americans go where no man has gone before; Canadians follow hoping to make that new place livable.**
>
> *—Michael Adams, Fire and Ice: The United States, Canada and the Myth of Converging Values, 2003*

The textile mills closed, ethnic Catholic churches emptied, and people left French Canadian neighborhoods for homes in the suburbs. This change is reflected in census statistics. In 2000 fewer people identified themselves as French Canadian than in the past. For example, 23 percent of Maine's 1.3 million residents reported that their origin was either French or French Canadian, a decrease from 27 percent in the 1990 census. Also, few of them speak French. Most of those who do are elderly or live close to the border.

In spite of these changes, French Canadian culture does live on. Many Franco-Americans are interested in researching their family's ancestry. Others are trying to keep the culture alive by organizing community activities. These include music

A Cajun band offers a concert in downtown Lafayette, Louisiana.

festivals or writing newspaper columns describing the community's heritage. Researching and teaching Franco-American history in schools and colleges offers another way to preserve the culture.

Franco-Americans of Cajun ancestry strive to maintain their heritage as well. Some aspects of Cajun culture have survived in the twenty-two parishes (counties) of Louisiana known as Acadiana, where many people are descended from the original Acadian exiles. People in some small Acadiana towns tell old folktales and go hunting for crawfish along the bayous (a traditional Cajun activity). Others maintain historic and cultural exhibits that educate tourists and schoolchildren about Acadian history. Meanwhile, lively Cajun music is popular across North America. So is Cajun cooking. Spicy seafood dishes such as jambalaya and gumbo (soup) can be found in many places throughout the United States.

> MANY PEOPLE ARE INTERESTED IN LEARNING ABOUT THEIR FAMILY'S HISTORY. THIS STUDY IS CALLED GENEALOGY. IF YOU'D LIKE TO LEARN ABOUT YOUR OWN GENEALOGY AND HOW YOUR ANCESTORS CAME TO AMERICA, VISIT WWW.INAMERICABOOKS.COM FOR TIPS AND LINKS TO HELP YOU GET STARTED.

FINDING SUCCESS IN THE UNITED STATES

Canadian immigrants of every ethnic background are highly motivated to succeed in the United States. They strive to maintain their heritage while making their way in their new homes. For many Canadians, the American dream is within reach. That dream suggests that anyone, regardless of background, can

Blood has never been the main American definition because her blood comes from everywhere. . . .

—Robert McNeil, Canadian immigrant and television journalist, from his book Looking for My Country: Finding Myself in America, 2004

achieve success through hard work and determination.

Twenty-first-century Canadian immigrants are still pursing the American dream. But the number of Canadians who move to the United States each year is not as large as it once was. Out of a population of approximately 31 million, 19,500 Canadian-born individuals immigrated to the United States annually in the early twenty-first century. From Canada's viewpoint, this loss is significant. Most of those who leave are well educated, earn high salaries, and are in the most productive years of their lives. Although many skilled immigrants from around the world arrive in Canada each year, Canadians still worry about the brain drain. From the U.S. standpoint, however, Canadian immigration is a positive phenomenon. It contributes valuable skills to the United States.

Whether large or small, waves of Canadian immigrants will continue to arrive in the United States. They will continue to contribute generously to their new home, and their children and grandchildren will form new generations of Americans.

Famous Canadian Americans

Paul Anka (b. 1941) This singer and songwriter was born in Ottawa. He became a teen idol in the 1950s and 1960s. He started performing at the age of twelve. His first hit, released in 1957, was "Diana," a song he wrote about his babysitter. Other hit songs include "Put Your Head on My Shoulder" and "Puppy Love." He also wrote "She's A Lady" for entertainer Tom Jones, and rewrote "My Way" for the famous singer Frank Sinatra.

Elizabeth Arden (1884–1966) Born Florence Nightingale Graham in Toronto, this cosmetics executive moved to New York around 1908. She started as an assistant to a beauty specialist, and in 1910 became a partner in a Fifth Avenue beauty salon. After the partnership split up, she continued the business, calling it Elizabeth Arden. In 1914 she hired some chemists to create new creams and lotions. Her line of cosmetics eventually included about three hundred products. Arden was an exceptional businessperson at a time when most women did not work outside the home.

Leo Durocher (1905–1991) This baseball player and manager, born in West Springfield, Massachusetts, was a well-known Franco-American. He became famous while playing for the Saint Louis Cardinals in 1934. He managed the Brooklyn Dodgers from 1939–1946 but was suspended for the 1947 season. Later, he managed the New York Giants, the Chicago Cubs, and the Houston Astros. He was known for his win-at-all-costs attitude and for stating, "Nice guys finish last."

Michael J. Fox (b. 1961) This actor was born in Edmonton, Alberta. He got his first professional acting job in Vancouver when he was fifteen. He moved to Los Angeles to pursue an acting career at eighteen. He appeared in the sitcom *Family Ties* through the 1980s and in many movies, including the Back to the Future series. He retired from the television show *Spin City* in

web enhanced at www.inamericabooks.com

2000 after announcing that he has Parkinson's disease, a condition that affects the nervous system. Fox has raised millions of dollars for research into this disease.

FRANK O. GEHRY (b. 1929)

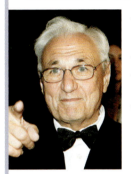

Acclaimed architect Frank O. Gehry was born in Toronto. He graduated from the University of Southern California in 1954 and opened his own architectural firm in 1962. He is both a sculptor and an architect. Gehry designed the Guggenheim Museum in Bilbao, Spain; the Walt Disney Concert Hall in Los Angeles, California; and the Weisman Art Museum in Minneapolis, Minnesota.

MEL GOODES (b. 1935)

Born in Hamilton, Ontario, Goodes worked at part-time jobs starting at the age of ten to help make ends meet at home. He studied at Queen's University in Kingston, Ontario, and at the University of Chicago. In 1965 he got a job in the Canadian office of Warner-Lambert, a worldwide manufacturer of prescription drugs and consumer products. He moved to the main office in New Jersey and headed the company until his retirement in 1999. Goodes has given money to various causes and institutions, including Queen's University.

WAYNE GRETZKY (b. 1961)

Born in Brantford, Ontario, Gretzky learned to play hockey on a rink in his family's backyard. During his National Hockey League

career, he broke more than sixty records. He played for five teams, including the Edmonton Oilers and the Los Angeles Kings. He retired as a player in 1999. In 2002 Gretsky managed Canada's men's hockey team in the Winter Olympics in Salt Lake City, Utah. The team won a gold medal. In 2005 Gretzky embarked on another stage of his hockey career. He became head coach of the Phoenix Coyotes.

Peter Jennings (1938–2005)

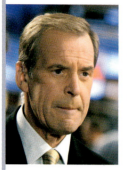

Born in Toronto, Jennings started his career as a disc jockey and reporter for a small private radio station. He received considerable attention for his coverage of a train wreck. He then got a job with a national Canadian television network. In 1964 he joined the U.S. television network ABC. He worked as a news anchor and as a foreign correspondent. He became anchor of ABC's Nightly News broadcast in 1983. He remained in that position through 2005, when he announced that he had lung cancer. Jennings died at the age of 67, just months after his cancer diagnosis.

Jack Kerouac (1922–1969)

Born in Lowell, Massachusetts, author Jean-Louis (Jack) Kerouac spoke only French until he was six years old. His parents were both Franco-Americans. In 1949 he and a friend drove across the United States. This trip provided material for his most famous book, *On the Road*, published in 1957. He was one of the best-known Beat Generation writers. He did not like celebrity and died at age 47 of an alcohol-related disease.

Calixa Lavallée (1842–1891)

Born in Verchères, Quebec, Lavallée was a musician. During the Civil War, he enlisted with a Rhode Island regiment and was discharged after being wounded. He returned to Quebec, where he wrote the music for a French Canadian patriotic song, "O Canada." He later moved to Boston, where he taught music at Carlyle Petersilea Music Academy, acted as choirmaster at the Roman Catholic Cathedral of the Holy Cross, and became a respected composer. More than 100 years after he wrote it, "O Canada" became Canada's national anthem.

MIKE MYERS

(b. 1963) This actor and screenwriter was born in Toronto, the son of British immigrants. The day he graduated from high school, he auditioned for a Toronto comedy troupe. Myers became a writer and performer on the television show *Saturday Night Live* in 1989. He took one of his television characters, Wayne Campbell, to the movie screen in *Wayne's World*. Myers also wrote, produced, and starred in the film *Austin Powers*, as well as its sequels.

JAMES A. NAISMITH

(1861–1939) Naismith is best known for inventing the game of basketball. A son of Scottish immigrants, he was born in Almonte, Ontario. As a child, Naismith showed promise as an athlete. In 1890 he went to a YMCA college in Springfield, Massachusetts, to train as a youth leader. There he invented basketball. Naismith eventually became a doctor and taught medicine at the University of Kansas for many years. He also maintained his interest in physical education.

MARY PICKFORD

(1893–1979) This movie star was known as "America's sweetheart." Born Gladys Mary Smith in Toronto, she started acting at the age of five. In Hollywood Pickford starred in many silent films, usually playing an innocent young girl. A good businessperson, she helped found United Artists Corporation. She and her husband, Douglas Fairbanks, were famous for the parties they held in their Hollywood mansion. In 1929 Pickford won an Academy Award for her first talking movie. She retired from acting in 1933 but continued as a writer and producer.

E. Annie Proulx (b. 1935)

Proulx was born in Norwich, Connecticut. She was the daughter of a Franco-American who worked in a textile mill as a boy and rose to vice president of his company. Proulx grew up in mill towns across New England and North Carolina. She attended Colby College in Maine, the University of Vermont, and Concordia University in Montreal. She later became a freelance journalist and founded a small-town newspaper in Vermont. When Proulx was in her fifties, she realized that what she really wanted to do was to write fiction. In 1994 she received the Pulitzer Prize for her novel *The Shipping News*.

Caroline Rhea (b. 1964)

Born in Montreal, Rhea wanted to be in show business from an early age. She went to New York City to learn stand-up comedy in 1989 and performed in a number of comedy clubs. She moved to Los Angeles in 1996 to play Aunt Hilda on the hit television program *Sabrina the Teenage Witch*. She has acted in many other television shows and movies, appeared regularly on *Hollywood Squares*, and hosted a talk show.

Jeffrey Skoll (b. 1965)

Skoll became wealthy as one of the founders of the Internet auction site eBay, but he is making his mark through charitable giving. Born in Montreal, Skoll studied electrical engineering at the University of Toronto, then went to Stanford University in California to study business. A friend asked him to help set up an online marketplace, and Skoll became president of eBay. He left that position in 1999 to establish the Skoll Foundation. The Skoll Foundation helps people around the world create new approaches to solving social problems in their communities.

RICHARD E. TAYLOR (b. 1929) This Nobel Prize–winning physicist was born in Medicine Hat, Alberta. He attended the University of Alberta in Edmonton, where he studied physics. He and his wife went to California, where he attended graduate school at Stanford University. He then spent three years doing research in France. He returned to the United States in 1961 and conducted research at the Stanford Linear Accelerator Center. In 1990 he and two colleagues won the Nobel Prize for their studies of the scattering of electrons.

SHIRLEY TILGHMAN (b.1946)

This molecular biologist became president of Princeton University in 2001. She is the first woman to head the university in its 255-year history and the second Canadian in a row to do so. (She succeeded Canadian-born Harold Shapiro.) Born in Toronto, Tilghman attended college in Canada and the United States, then taught school in West Africa for two years. She has been at Princeton since 1986. Her research career focused on the genetics of mammals.

Timeline

C.A. 50,000 B.C.	Migrants from Asia arrive in Canada and begin spreading across North America.
1497	British explorer John Cabot travels to North America.
1541	French explorer Jacques Cartier and his men spend a winter near present-day Quebec City.
1608	French explorer Samuel de Champlain builds a fort at present-day Quebec City.
1663–1673	*Les filles du roi* (the king's daughters) arrive in New France to marry the European merchants, soldiers, and other men who are already there. They begin raising families.
1701	A group of French and French Canadian voyageurs establish an outpost on the Detroit River that will eventually become Detroit.
1713	The British take over Acadia and rename it Nova Scotia.
1754	The French and Indian War begins.
1755	The British begin to expel thousands of Acadians from their homes.
1763	France hands over all of its North American territory east of the Mississippi River to Britain.
1764	The first small group of Acadians arrive at the port of New Orleans.
1774	The British parliament passes the Quebec Act.
1775	The American Revolution begins. American settlers hope the Canadiens will fight the British.

web enhanced at www.inamericabooks.com

1783	The Treaty of Paris, the agreement that ends the American Revolution, is signed.
1791	Britain splits Quebec into two separate colonies, Upper Canada and Lower Canada.
1812	The United States declares war on the British.
1815	The United States signs the Treaty of Ghent, ending the War of 1812.
1840	Upper Canada and Lower Canada together become the Province of Canada. At about the same time, thousands of British and French Canadians begin to immigrate to the United States.
1846	The Oregon Treaty settles a dispute over the border location in the west.
1860–1900	French Canadian immigration to the United States peaks.
1867	Nova Scotia, New Brunswick, and the Province of Canada join to form the Dominion of Canada.
1870	The first French-language parochial school opens in Rutland, Vermont.
1876	Alexander Graham Bell sends the first telephone message in Boston. He came up with the idea for the telephone two years before while visiting his parents in Ontario. He was born in Scotland and lived in Canada before moving to th United States.
1885	The Canadian Pacific Railroad is completed from Montreal to the Pacific Ocean.

1933	Canadian-born cartoonist Joe Shuster and writer Jerry Siegel create the comic book hero Superman in Cleveland, Ohio.
1939	World War II begins, and Canadian immigration to the United States slows.
1947	The Canadian Citizenship Act is passed. Prior to this, Canadians were considered British subjects.
1965	The United States limits the number of annual immigrants from each country to twenty thousand individuals.
1968	The state of Louisiana establishes the Council for the Development of French in Louisiana (CODOFIL).
1982	The Canadian government patriates, or brings home, its constitution from the British Parliament and introduces the Canadian Charter of Rights and Freedoms.
1993	E. Annie Proulx's Pulitzer Prize–winning novel, *The Shipping News*, is published.
1994	The North American Free Trade Agreement (NAFTA) goes into effect.
2005	The U.S. Department of Homeland Security announces that, as of December 31, 2006, Canadians and returning U.S. travelers will need passports to cross the border by sea or air. Those crossing the U.S.–Canadian border by land will need passports as of December 31, 2007.

Glossary

ABORIGINAL: the first people in a particular region. North America's aboriginal people are also referred to as Native Americans, Indians, or First Nations people.

ALLIES: people with a bond or a connection. Allies can be individuals, states, or groups of people.

COLONY: a territory that is tied to or controlled by another country

HERITAGE: something possessed as a result of one's situation or birth. Heritage includes all of the traditions and customs associated with a particular culture.

IMMIGRATE: to come to live in a country other than one's homeland. A person who immigrates is called an immigrant.

MERCHANT: a businessperson or trader

MIGRANT: a person who moves from one region to another

MILITIA: a group of citizens organized for military service

MISSIONARY: a person on a religious mission, generally to promote a particular religion

NEUTRAL: not taking either side

PAROCHIAL: of or relating to a church

TREATY: an agreement in writing between two or more political authorities (such as countries)

VOYAGEUR: A fur company employee who hauls goods to and from remote places

Things to See and Do

**ACADIAN MEMORIAL,
SAINT MARTINVILLE, LOUISIANA**
http://www.acadianmemorial.org/British/index.html
The Acadian Memorial includes a painted mural of the Acadian refugees arriving in Louisiana, as well as a wall with the names of three thousand of the exiles. Local actors depict scenes from the lives of the transplanted Acadians.

**CADILLAC STATUE,
DETROIT, MICHIGAN**
http://fchsm.habitant.org/#plaque
This statue of Antoine Lamothe-Cadillac (1658–1730) in Hart Plaza, Detroit, recalls the French-born fur trader and military officer. In 1701 Cadillac established the first permanent settlement at Detroit. An adjacent plaque honors the fifty-one French Canadian voyageurs who accompanied him.

**LONGFELLOW-EVANGELINE STATE HISTORIC SITE,
SAINT MARTINVILLE, LOUISIANA**
http://www.crt.state.la.us/crt/parks/longfell/longfell.htm
This historic site marks the spot where Acadian exiles arrived in 1764. It features an Acadian-style rustic cabin, a typical Acadian farmstead, and a plantation house.

**MUSEUM OF WORK AND CULTURE,
WOONSOCKET, RHODE ISLAND**
http://www.ci.woonsocket.ri.us/museum.htm
This museum is operated by the Rhode Island Historical Society. Through hundreds of photos and other exhibits, it presents the story of the French Canadians who left their farms in Quebec for the factories of New England.

**PERE MARQUETTE STATE PARK,
GRAFTON, ILLINOIS**
http://www.greatriverroad.com/Pere/PereIndex.htm
This park, at the junction of the Illinois and Mississippi rivers, covers about eight thousand acres. It is named after Father Jacques Marquette. This missionary accompanied French Canadian explorer Louis Jolliet as he followed the Mississippi River to the mouth of the Arkansas River in 1673. A stone cross in the park marks the spot where the mouth of the Illinois was probably located in Jolliet's lifetime.

Source Notes

16   R. Douglas Francis, Richard Jones, and Donald B. Smith, *Origins: Canadian History to Confederation* (Toronto: Holt, Rinehart and Winston of Canada, 1988), 165.

22   Henry Wadsworth Longfellow, *Evangeline*, (ND) http://www.classicreader.com/read.php/sid.4/bookid.146/sec.8/ (May 4, 2005).

26   John Herd Thompson and Stephen J. Randall, *Canada and the United States: Ambivalent Allies*, 3rd ed. (Athens: The University of Georgia Press, 2002), 52.

29   Rhea Côté Robbins, *Wednesday's Child* (Brewer, ME: Rheta Press, 2001), 49.

47   Jeffrey Simpson, *Star-Spangled Canadians: Canadians Living the American Dream* (Toronto: HarperCollins, 2000), 47.

48   Kathleen Fell, telephone interview with author, May 12, 2004.

49   Robin Dosonge, telephone interview with author, May 15, 2004.

50   Michael Adams, *Fire and Ice: The United States, Canada and the Myth of Converging Values* (Toronto: Penguin Canada, 2003), 123.

53   Robert McNeil, *Looking for My Country: Finding Myself in America* (Toronto: Random House, 2002), 7.

Selected Bibliography

Adams, Michael. *Fire and Ice: The United States, Canada and the Myth of Converging Values*. Toronto: Penguin Canada, 2003. **This award-winning book by the president of a public opinion research firm examines the differences between the beliefs that Canadians and Americans hold.**

Belanger, Claude. "French Canadian Emigration to the United States, 1840–1930." Quebec History (Marionopolis College), August 23, 2000 http://www2.marianopolis.edu/quebechistory/readings/leaving.htm (April 21, 2005). **This website provides an excellent overview of the reasons why people left Quebec, their living conditions in the United States, and the process of becoming part of U.S. society.**

Bradshaw, Jim. "Culture, Not Blood, Defines Today's Cajun." *Lafayette: Genuine Cajun. Uniquely Creole.* (lafayettetravel.com), reprinted from *Lafayette Daily Advertiser* (ND) http://www.lafayettetravel.com/culture/history/what_is_cajun.cfm (April 21, 2005) **This article examines the culture of the Cajun community.**

Brasseaux, Carl A. *Acadian to Cajun: Transformation of a People, 1803–1877*. Jackson: University Press of Mississippi, 1992. **This book describes how the Acadian people who came from Nova Scotia became the Cajun people of Louisiana.**

Brault, Gerard J. *The French Canadian Heritage in New England*. Hanover, NH: University Press of New England, 1986. **This book tells the story of French Canada and the people who left it to work in the factories of New England.**

The Canadian Encyclopedia. April 21, 2005 http://www.thecanadianencyclopedia.com (April 21, 2005). **This useful Canadian resource, including both the standard and junior editions, originally appeared in print. The entire text is available online.**

DuLong, John P. French *Canadians in Michigan*. East Lansing: Michigan State University Press, 2001. **This volume is illustrated with numerous historical photos. It includes extensive notes and lists of other resources.**

Francis, R. Douglas, Richard Jones, and Donald B. Smith. *Origins: Canadian History to Confederation*. Toronto: Holt, Rinehart and Winston of Canada, 1988. **This Canadian history textbook examines Canada's origins and development.**

Lamarre, Jean. *The French Canadians of Michigan: Their Contribution to the Development of the Saginaw Valley and the Keweenaw Peninsula, 1840–1914*. Detroit: Wayne State University Press, 2003. **This book explores French Canadian migration to Michigan, from the fur trade to the twentieth century.**

Ramirez, Bruno. *Crossing the 49th Parallel. Migration from Canada to the United States 1900–1930*. Ithaca, NY: Cornell University Press, 2001. **This book discusses why so many French- and English-speaking Canadians left their homelands and what they experienced as they settled in the United States.**

Thompson, John Herd, and Stephen J. Randall. *Canada and the United States: Ambivalent Allies*. 3rd ed. Athens: The University of Georgia Press, 2002. **This book examines the relationship between Canada and the United States.**

Further Reading & Websites

Nonfiction

Arial, Tracey. *I Volunteered: Canadian Vietnam Vets Remember*. Winnipeg: Watson & Dwyer, 1996. **This book tells the stories of some of the Canadians who fought in the Vietnam War.**

Bial, Raymond. *Cajun Home*. Boston: Houghton Mifflin Co., 1998. **Photographs in this work illustrate the heritage of the Cajun people of Louisiana, while the text explains many of their traditional customs.**

Braun, Eric. *Canada in Pictures*. Minneapolis: Lerner Publications

Company, 2003. **Learn more about Canada in this book covering the country's history, geography, and culture.**

Coupland, Douglas. *Souvenir of Canada*. Vancouver: Douglas & McIntyre, 2002. **This title is one man's take on what it means to be Canadian. It addresses topics such as Canadians' love of hockey and their taste for french fries with vinegar.**

Laxer, James. *The Border: Canada, the U.S. and Dispatches from the 49th Parallel*. Toronto: Doubleday, 2003. **The author describes what the Canada-U.S. border looks like and who lives there. He also discusses the border's significance following the terrorist attacks of September 11, 2001.**

Lunn, Janet. *The Story of Canada*. 3rd ed. Toronto: Key Porter Books, 2000. **This book tells the story of Canada from the days of the dinosaurs to modern times.**

McNeil, Robert. *Looking for My Country. Finding Myself in America*. Toronto: Random House, 2002. **In this title, Canadian immigrant and television journalist Robert McNeil explores his feelings about Canada and the United States.**

Simpson, Jeffrey. *Star-Spangled Canadians: Canadians Living the American Dream*. Toronto: HarperCollins, 2000. **This book discusses the contemporary experiences of Canadians who live in the United States.**

FICTION

Hémon, Louis. *Maria Chapdelaine*. Translated by Alan Brown. Montreal: Tundra Books, 1989. **This classic of Quebec literature tells the story of a young woman who must decide whether to leave Canada or to stay in the land she loves.**

Lunn, Janet. *The Hollow Tree*. Toronto: A. Knopf Canada, 1997. **In this novel set during the American Revolution, fifteen-year-old Phoebe falls in love with a young Loyalist who is heading for Canada with his family.**

Pearson, Kit. *This Land*. Toronto: Viking, 1998. **This anthology of Canadian fiction includes short stories and excerpts from novels. The collection emphasizes a sense of place, from southern Ontario to the Arctic.**

Sutherland, Robert. *A River Apart*. Markham, ON: Fitzhenry and Whiteside, 2000. James, a Loyalist teenager in Upper Canada, is separated from his American friends after the outbreak of the War of 1812. But when James is injured, his American friends take care of him.

WEBSITES

CBC ARCHIVES
http://archives.cbc.ca/index.asp?IDLan=1
This website has features on important people, events, and issues in Canadian history.

ENCYCLOPEDIA OF CAJUN CULTURE
http://www.cajunculture.com/
Visitors to this site will find articles on Cajun life, including well-known musicians, historical events, and places in Acadia.

INAMERICABOOKS.COM
http://www.inamericabooks.com
Visit www.inamericabooks.com, the online home of the In America series, to get linked to all sorts of useful information. You'll find historical and cultural websites related to individual groups, as well as general information on genealogy, creating your own family tree, and the history of immigration in America.

MAINE'S FRENCH COMMUNITIES
http://www.francomaine.org/index.htm
This website examines the history and current population of Maine's French communities.

OUR CANADIAN GIRL
http://ourcanadiangirl.ca/
Visit this site for activities based on the *Our Canadian Girl* series of novels. These titles for young people tell the stories of girls who come from different periods in Canadian history.

VIRTUAL MUSEUM OF CANADA
http://www.virtualmuseum.ca
Learn about Canada from exhibits put together by dozens of museums across the country. Topics range from life in Acadia to Canadian space ventures. You can also play a game or send a postcard to a friend.

INDEX

Acadia (also Acadie), 9, 12–16
Acadiana, 52
Acadians, 5, 60, 64: in Louisiana (as Cajuns), 22, 31, 52; in New England, 28–29; in Michigan, 30–31; removal of, 12–16
African American(s), 23, 36. *See also* slavery; Underground Railroad
Alaska, 7, 8; and Alaska Panhandle, 21
American Revolutionary War, 4, 16–20, 60; and Treaty of Paris, 19

Britain, 14, 16, 22, 23, 24, 60, 61
British, 4–5, 8, 11–16, 17–20, 24, 25

Cabot, John, 8, 60
Cajuns, 22, 31. 35, 52. *See also* Acadians
California, 35, 38, 48, 55, 58, 59
Canada, 2, 3, 27, 28, 30, 32, 34, 37, 53, 55, 56, 59, 60, 61; Dominion of Canada, 25, 61; early history of, 6–9; early 1900s, 26; as "fifty-first state," 45; French and Indian War, 14–16; Lower Canada, 20, 22; New France, 10–12; Quebec Act and the American Revolution, 18–20; removal of Acadians from, 12–16; traditions, traits, and values, 46–47, 50; Upper Canada, 19, 20, 22; and U.S. Civil War, 24–26; U.S. emigration to, 37–38, 39, 42; and War of 1812, 20, 61; World War I, 32–33; World War II, 34, 61
Canadian Americans; Canadiens, 11–12, 14, 18; and clubs of, 41; descent of, 17, 20, 22, 26, 28–31, 34, 35, 43, 49, 50–52, 54, 56, 60, 61; famous, 54–59; foods of, 43, 44; holidays of, 30, 36, 42–43, 46, 49; and patriotism, 46, 56; and protest, 47; religions (faiths) of, 10, 12, 22, 30, 51, 56; settlement of, 6, 12, 14–20, 24–25, 26, 36–39, 44, 45, 49, 51, 55, 57, 61. *See also* Canada: early history of; traditions, traits, and values of, 30, 42, 43, 46–47, 50, 52; and work (careers, jobs, and labor), 24, 25–26, 31–34, 38–39, 40, 45, 48, 49, 52, 54–59
Canadian Pacific Railroad, 25, 61
Carrey, Jim, 41. *See also* famous Canadian Americans
Cartier, Jacques, 8–9, 58
Champlain, Samuel de, 10–11, 60
Civil War, U.S., 24–26; Canadians serving in, 25
Columbus, Christopher, 4
Customs and Immigration, 45

English (language), 5, 16, 28, 30, 31, 34–35, 39
Europe, 27, 32, 35, 40
Europeans, 9, 10, 12, 32

famous Canadian Americans, 54–59
France, 8, 9, 10, 14, 16, 59, 60
Franco-Americans, 50–52, 54
French (language), 5, 12, 16–17, 22, 28. 29, 30, 31, 35, 50, 56, 61, 62
French Canadians, 17, 20, 22, 26, 28–31, 34, 35, 43, 49, 50–51, 56, 60, 61

Great Depression, 34_35
Great Lakes, the, 12, 30

Halifax, Nova Scotia, 13, 14, 27
Hudson's Bay Company, 11–12

immigrants and immigration, 20, 23, 26, 27, 28–31, 32–35, 40–43, 47, 50, 52–53, 55, 57, 61; and the Erie Canal, 20; and the Grand Trunk Railway, 22; stories of, 48–49; trends of, 36–39; and U.S. Department of Homeland Security, 45, 62; U.S. Immigration Service, 27; U.S. Senate commission immigration report, 31–32; waves of, 4–5, 20, 22–23, 24–26, 28–30, 31–35, 37–39, 40–43

Jolliet, Louis, 12

La Salle, René-Robert Cavelier de, 12
Lavallée, Calixa, 26. *See also* famous Canadians
Little Canada (*p'tit Canada*, Frenchville), 29
Loyalists, 19. *See also* American Revolution

maps, 17, 33

Native Americans, 4, 7–9, 11–12, 14, 20, 32, 63

Quebec: colony of: 16–18, 20; province of, 9, 25, 28–29, 37, 43. *See also* Canada: early history
Quebec Act, 16–17, 60
Quebec City, 10, 16, 18, 27, 60

recipe: bannock, 44

Saint John, New Brunswick, 13, 19, 27
slavery, 23, 24, 25. *See also* Underground Railroad
South America, 8
Spain, 8, 16, 55
sports: baseball, 54; hockey, 42, 48, 55
Sweden, 27

Toronto, Ontario, 6, 42, 50, 54, 55, 56, 57, 58
traditions, traits, and values, *See* Canadian Americans

Ukraine, 32
Underground Railroad. *See also* slavery
United States, 4–5, 6–7, 19, 20, 21, 22–23; and Civil War years, 24–26; early 1900s, 26, 28; and French Canadians, 28–30, 31–35; life in, 4, 5, 8, 22, 35, 39–43, 45, 48, 50; and mid-1900s to present, 36–37; and success in, 52–53; and values, 46–47, 50
U.S. Immigration Service. *See* immigrants and immigration

Vancouver, British Columbia, 6, 54
Vietnam War, 37

War of 1812, 20, 61
World War I, 32–33
World War II, 34, 61

Acknowledgments: The images in this book are used with the permission of: Digital Vision Royalty Free, pp. 1, 3, 24; Photo Disc Royalty Free by Getty Images, p. 6; Lyn Hancock, p. 7; Courtesy of the Peabody Essex Museum, p. 8; © Confederation Life Gallery of Canadian History, pp. 9, 19; Library of Congress, pp. 10, 21 (LC-USZC4-6092), 31 (LC-USZ62-93425), 48 (Haer, CAL,38-SanFRA,140-43), 57 (right) (LC-USZ62-057952); James Ford Bell Library, University of Minnesota, p. 11; National Archives of Canada/C-041605, p. 13; Collection of The Rooms, Provincial Museum Division, p. 14; © Bettmann/CORBIS, pp. 15, 37, 38, 56 (bottom); Bill Hauser, pp. 17, 33; © The Granger Collection, New York, p. 18; © North Wind Picture Archives, p. 20; © Keystone-Mast Collection, UCR/California Museum of Photography, University of California at Riverside, p. 28; National Archives, W & C 0635, p. 32; Saskatchewan Archives Board, p. 34 (R-B9523); © Todd Strand/Independent Picture Service, p. 40; Photofest, pp. 41, 57 (left); Jon Adams/Icon SMI, p. 42; © Walter and Louisann Pietrowicz/September 8th Stock, p. 43; © Reuters/CORBIS, p. 47; © Phillip Gould/CORBIS, p. 51; © Tina Fulta/ZUMA Press, p. 54; © Carlo Allegri/Getty Images for LAPA, p. 55 (left); © Stan Liu/Icon SMI/ZUMA Press, p. 55 (right); © Nancy Kaszerman/ZUMA Press, p. 56 (top); © Chris Delmas/ZUMA Press, p. 58 (top); © Lori Conn/ZUMA Press, p. 58 (bottom); Denise Applewhite/Princeton University Office of Communications, p. 59.

Front cover: Digital Vision Royalty Free (title); © John Kelly/Image Bank/Getty Images (center); Photo Disc Royalty Free by Getty Images (bottom). Back cover: Digital Vision Royalty Free.